A Silent Night for

by Tom Hegg
illustrated by Warren Hanson

Waldman House Press, Inc.

For Peggy, without whom…
T.H.

For Patty, a very big part of every little thing I do.
W.H.

Library of Congress Cataloging-in-Publication Data
Hegg, Tom.
    A Silent Night for Peef / by Tom Hegg ; illustrated
by Warren Hanson.
        p.   cm.
    Summary: On Christmas Eve, Santa returns to visit
the multicolored teddy bear that he had made by hand
the year before and finds him well worn and well loved.
    ISBN 0-931674-35-2 (HC : alk. paper)
    [1. Teddy bears–Fiction. 2. Santa Claus–Fiction.
3. Christmas–Fiction. 4. Stories in rhyme.]
I. Hanson, Warren, ill. II. Title.
PZ8.3.H398Si 1998
[E]–dc21   98-35721

Waldman House Press, Inc.
525 North Third Street
Minneapolis, Minnesota 55401

Another Christmas Eve had come.

The waiting sleigh was full.

And Santa took the reins in hand and felt the reindeer pull.

The harness bells began to jingle as they gathered speed,

And whoosh! They took the frosty air,
with Blitzen in the lead.

They made their magic rounds again, like all the years before,

And brought the merry signs of Christmas cheer to every door.

And then, before that old familiar turn just north of Nome,

Old Santa said, "There's one more stop before we head for home."

The sleigh alighted on a humble roof… the very last

Before this Christmas Present would become a Christmas Past.

And in that home, Dear Children, lived a child who loved a bear.

A very special bear, indeed… a bear who was somewhere

Within the tangle of the sheets and blankets on a bed.

A multicolored bear of blue and green and brown and red.

A masterpiece that Santa Claus had made by hand. In brief,

The little teddy bear who bore the happy name of Peef.

To hear that sound just once again would be a precious gift.

He only had to find the little teddy bear and lift

Him up and touch his tummy, and a "peef" would be right there,

Just as it was when Santa Claus had made the little bear.

The child was sleeping lightly, as you might on Christmas Eve.

A toss… a turn… and there! Beside a blue pajama sleeve,
Dear Santa saw a paw he knew as well as his own hand,

And he grew so excited, it was all that he could stand

To keep from laughing right out loud (but this was Silent Night,

So ho-ho-ho-ing had to be postponed). A silver light

Began to filter through the windowpane, and Santa's eyes

Could see as clearly as they do in sparkling starlit skies.

The child turned again… and sure enough! Upon the sheet,
He saw the little bear right from his head down to his feet!

But there was something different. Peef had changed, and it was clear

Peef wasn't what he was when Santa left him here last year.

For he was dirty here… and here… and faded there… and there…

His right side had a little rip… the left a little tear…

When Santa touched Peef's tummy, he was stunned beyond belief —

The little bear sprang back to life, but could no longer peef!

They hugged each other tightly, they had missed each other so.

They read each other's thoughts, and Santa thought, "I ought to sew

You up a bit, and get you nice and clean again. I think

It won't take long to get your colors back into the pink.

And maybe I've an extra button somewhere in the sleigh

So you can have your voice again. It could be there's a way

To keep you safe from all the harm and danger waiting right

Around the corner for a teddy bear both day and night.

There must be… MUST be something else that I can do for you.

I know I'll think of something if I only think it through…"

But Peef broke into Santa's over-worried, hurried mind,
And said, "Dear Santa, please... you really mustn't try to find
A way to keep me safe from every single little thing.

I've seen a summer   and a fall,

a winter

and a spring.

You can't believe the fun I've had.

You can't believe the joy!

And if I've burst my seams a bit,

Well, so would any toy.

My days begin and end right here — right in this very bed.

I stay beside my little friend way up here at the head.

On school days, we get up and have our breakfast done by eight.

The bus comes right on time, and so we mustn't make them wait.

On Saturdays and Sundays, we can take our time and play

Because we don't get going until later in the day.

I wear a cape sometimes…
It goes on with a safety pin,
And that explains the little tear
You see beneath my chin.
I fly across the room…
Go sliding down the banister.

I ride the vacuum cleaner right astride the canister.

When Mom and Dad go to the store, we go along and start
To giggle when we feel a wheel wiggle on our cart.

One time, we went exploring, and I got to be a scout…

One time, we got in trouble and we had to have Time Out.

We go to church, and when we do, I always love to see

The windows, 'cause they're lots of colors, just the same as me.

Why, I've been in a treehouse.

I've been playing in the mud.

And I've been in a rowboat make-believing Noah's flood.

We made a castle out of chairs, and I became a Knight.

A dragon almost got me!

(Just pretend, so it's all right.)

Why, I've been in a backpack,

And I've been to school as well…

In fact, I even was the special guest for 'show-and-tell'.

I've jumped into a pile of leaves...

I've ridden on a bike…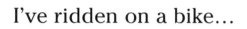

I've hidden in a box for 'hide-and-seek'.

We took a hike.

We had a picnic where we picked some flowers just for fun.

And we were there for hours, and we saw the setting sun.

I've seen so many colors… winter, summer, spring and fall,

But the greatest and most wonderful and special thing of all

Is something you can't see or hear or smell or taste or feel.

And it's only make-believe, but it's the only thing that's real…

It's knowing who you are, and being where you ought to be,

And doing what you ought to do…

and you gave that to me.

So you don't have to fix me up, for there is nothing wrong.

I'm just what I should be right now. I'm right where I belong.

And if I have a tear or two, or if I've lost my voice,

It doesn't matter. I'm the bear I should be. It's my choice.

And if I don't exactly last forever? Nothing does…

What will be will be. What is just is. What was just was."

And Santa laughed a silent laugh upon the Silent Night,

And then a cloud blew overhead and took the silver light.

He held the little teddy bear he'd made so long ago

With bits of cloth from all the elves, content from head to toe.

So Santa's finger pointed toward the tummy of the bear,

And then he thought, "Now, all I need to do is touch once — there."

And as he turned to go, he heard, upon the Silent Night,

a silent "peef" — and knew that all was calm, and all was right.